Little Cloud

For Sarton and Anjelica Tao

PUFFIN BOOKS
Published by the Penguin Group
Penguin Putnam Books for Young Readers, 345 Hudson Street, New York, New York 10014, U.S.A.
Penguin Books Ltd, 27 Wrights Lane, London W8 5TZ, England
Penguin Books Australia Ltd, Ringwood, Victoria, Australia
Penguin Books Canada Ltd, 10 Alcorn Avenue, Toronto, Ontario, Canada M4V 3B2
Penguin Books (N.Z.) Ltd, 182-190 Wairau Road, Auckland 10, New Zealand
Penguin Books Ltd, Registered Offices: Harmondsworth, Middlesex, England

First published in the United States of America by Philomel Books, a division of The Putnam & Grosset Group, 1996
Published by Puffin Books, a division of Penguin Putnam Books for Young Readers, 2001

10 9 8 7 6 5 4 3 2 1

THE LIBRARY OF CONGRESS HAS CATALOGED THE PHILOMEL EDITION AS FOLLOWS:
Carle, Eric. Little cloud / by Eric Carle. p. cm.
Summary: A little cloud becomes all sorts of things—sheep, an airplane, trees, a hat—before joining other clouds and raining.
ISBN 0-399-23034-3 [1. Clouds—Fiction.] I. Title.
PZ7.C21476Li 1996 [E]—dc20 95-38119 CIP AC

This edition ISBN 0-698-11830-8

Printed in Hong Kong
Set in Walbaum Bold

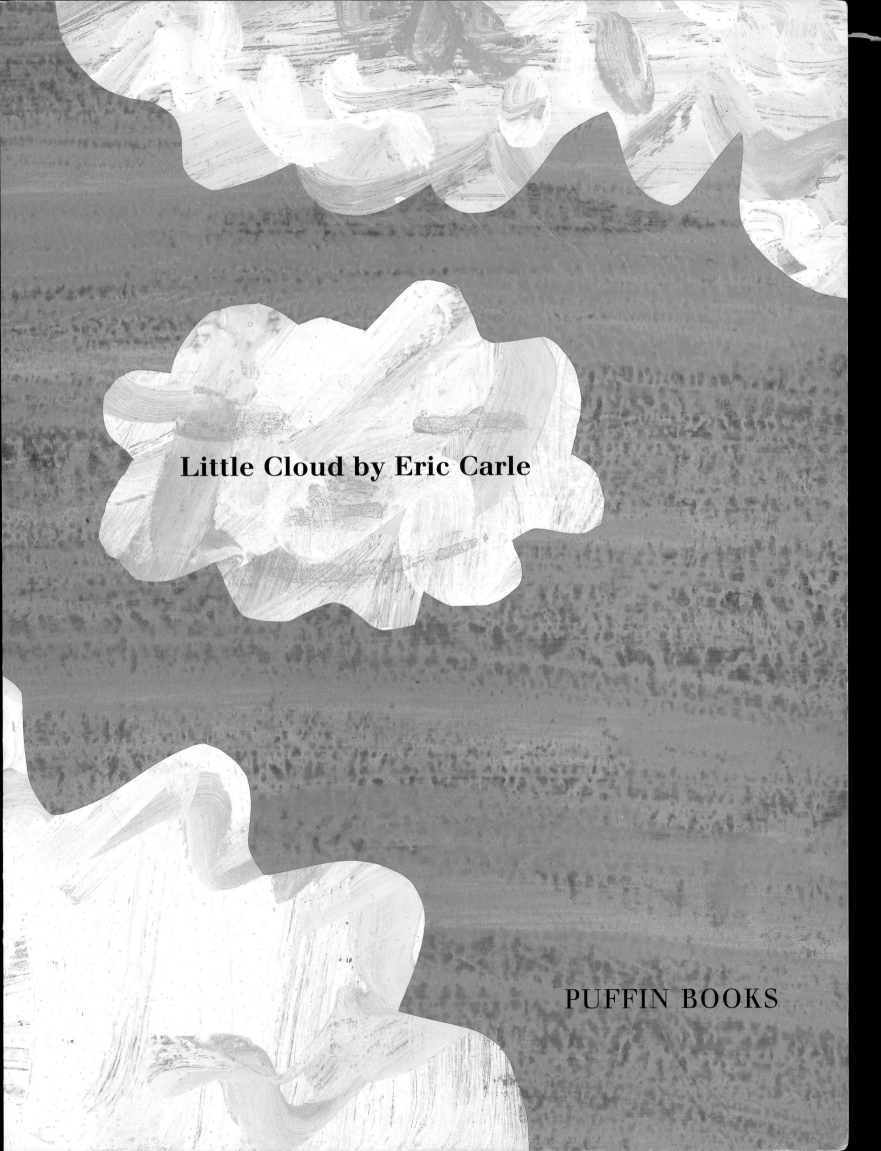

Little Cloud by Eric Carle

PUFFIN BOOKS

The clouds drifted slowly across the sky.
Little Cloud trailed behind.

The clouds pushed upward and away.
Little Cloud pushed downward and
touched the tops of the houses and trees.

The clouds moved out of sight.
Little Cloud changed into a giant cloud.

Little Cloud changed into a sheep.
Sheep and clouds sometimes look alike.

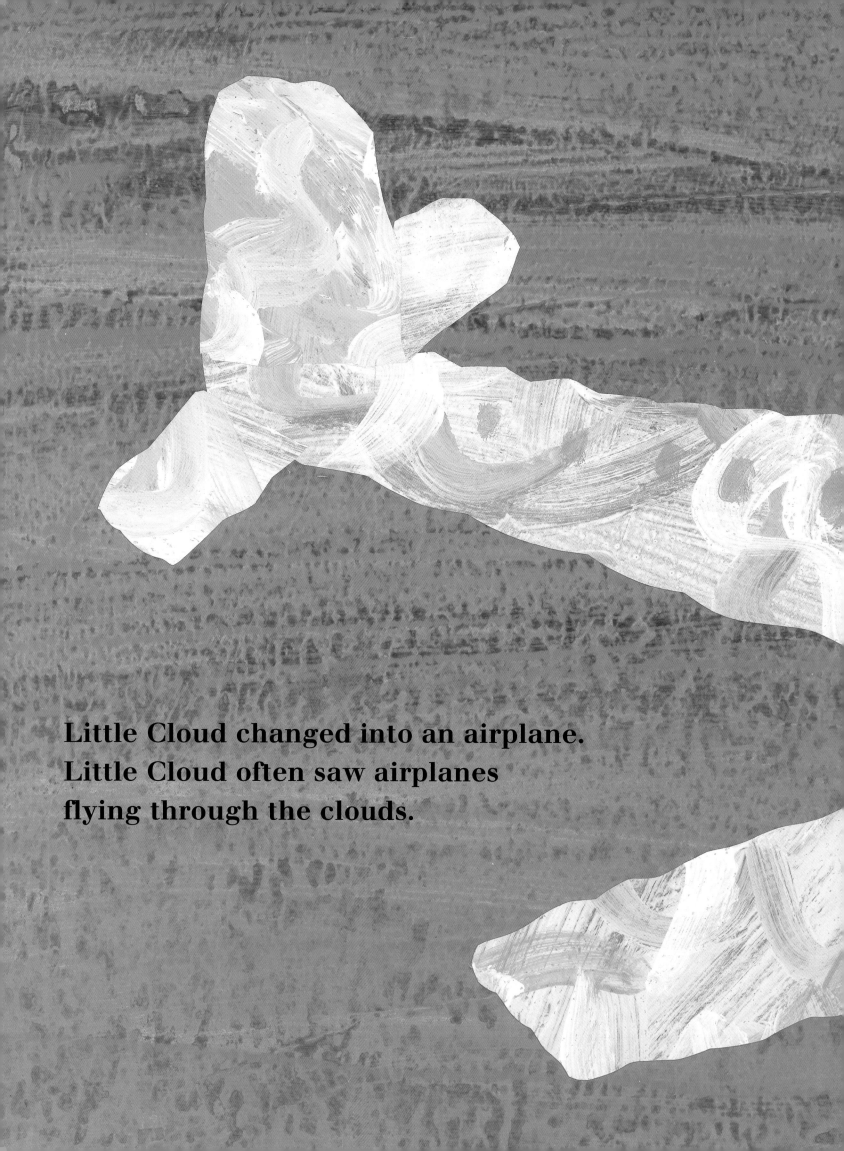

Little Cloud changed into an airplane.
Little Cloud often saw airplanes
flying through the clouds.

Little Cloud changed into a shark.
Little Cloud once saw a shark
through the waves of the ocean.

Little Cloud changed into two trees.
Little Cloud liked the way trees never
moved and stayed in one place.

Little Cloud changed into a rabbit.
Little Cloud loved to watch rabbits
dash across the meadows.

Then Little Cloud changed into a hat. Because . . .

Little Cloud changed into a clown and needed a hat.

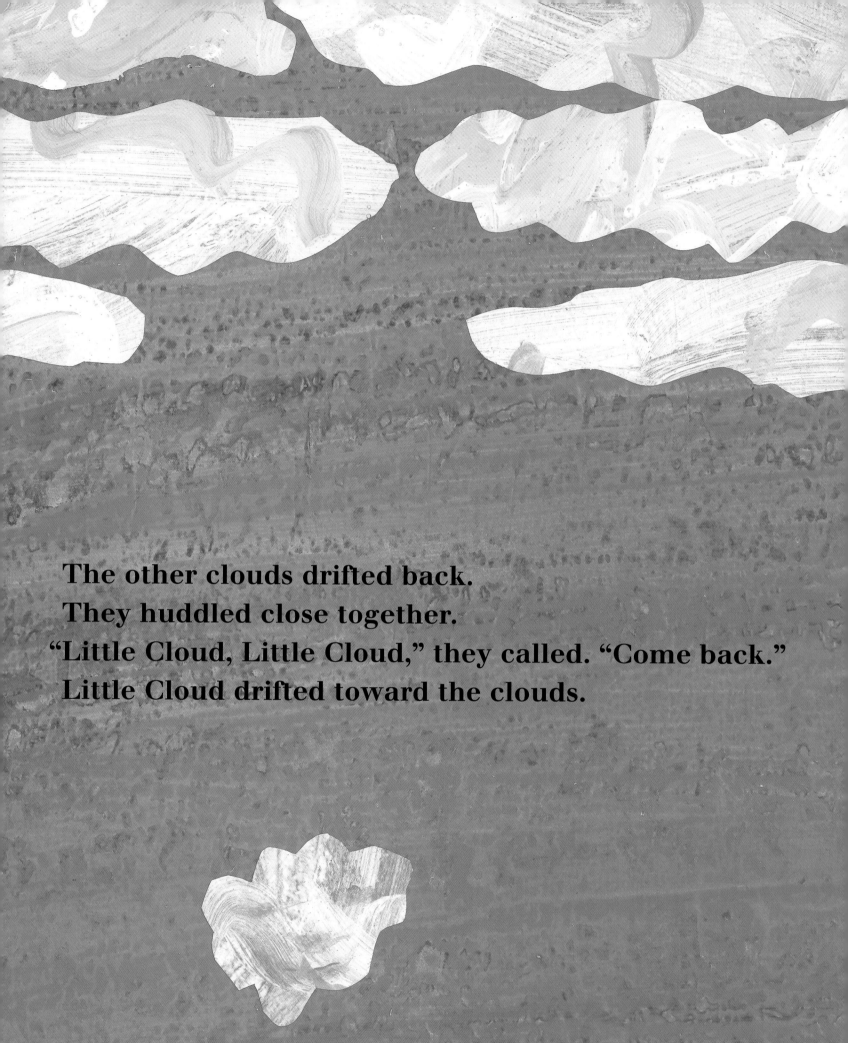

The other clouds drifted back.
They huddled close together.
"Little Cloud, Little Cloud," they called. "Come back."
Little Cloud drifted toward the clouds.

Then all the clouds changed into one big cloud and

rained!